KU-264-744

For James

Text copyright © Sally Grindley 1989
Illustrations copyright © Siobhan Dodds 1989

First published in Great Britain in 1989
by Simon & Schuster Ltd
Reprinted in 1991

Reprinted in 1997 by Macdonald Young Books
an imprint of Wayland Publishers Ltd
61 Western Road
Hove
East Sussex
BN3 1JD

This book is copyright under the Berne Convention.
No reproduction without permission in writing
from the publisher.

All rights reserved.

Printed in Hong Kong by Wing King Tong Co Ltd

British Library Cataloguing in Publication available

ISBN: 0 7500 0882 2

624316
MORAY COUNCIL
Department of Technical
& Leisure Services

CAN I HELP, DAD?

Sally Grindley

Illustrated by Siobhan Dodds

MacDonald Young Books

"Dad ... Can I help, Dad?"

"I'm good at painting, Mrs Powling says
so. I'll go and get my paints."

"Here they are, Dad."

"I've got lots of different colours. I've got more colours than you, Dad. You can borrow them if you want to."

"My favourite colour is purple. And
red's a nice colour, too, isn't it, Dad?
Red and purple look nice on white."

"Can I tear, too, Dad?"

"We do lots of tearing in Mrs Powling's
class. Jimmy tore up Susie's painting.
That was a naughty thing to do, wasn't it?"
"*Wheeee!* Look at my snowstorm, Dad."

"This is pretty paper, Dad. I like daisies.
Dandelions are my best flower. I like
blowing their tops off to tell the time."

"There must be lots of daisies on one
roll, mustn't there, Dad? Look how
long it is. Yum Yum's chasing it.
Look!"

"Yuch! What's that, Dad? It looks like
frog-spawn. Can you eat it?"

"It's ever so sticky, isn't it, Dad? Will it
stick to anything?"

"Look, Dad, look! Yum Yum's got some
stuck on her tail."

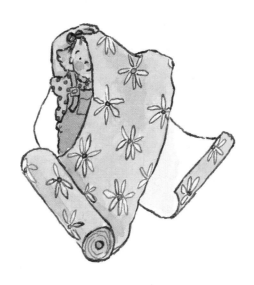

"Can I help, Dad? I know what to do."

"Oooo, hello, Dad!"

"My hair's gone all stiff and spiky, Dad.
I'm going to paint it pink so I look like
a pop star. Yum Yum would look nice
with pink fur, wouldn't she, Dad?"

"Dad, I'm bored, Dad."

"Have you nearly finished? Will you do jigsaws with me, Dad?"

"Look, Dad, look! Look at my monsters-from-outer-space stickers. They're ever so ugly. I've got dinosaurs, too. Do you think dinosaurs eat daisies, Dad?"

"Mind you don't fall, Dad! Jimmy's Dad fell off a ladder and broke his leg."

"Drip, drip, drip. The paint's dripping on the sheet, Dad. I'll pull it out of the way. Spots look nice, don't they, Dad? Mum likes spots. She's got lots of spotty dresses."

"Bump, bump, bump. My dumper truck
is coming to pick up the rubbish.
Bump, bump, bump. Beep, beep, Dad."

"That's Mum, Dad. Mum's back.
Mum, Mum, we're here!"

CRASH!

"Are you all right, Dad? Dad's been decorating, Mum, and I've been helping. I make a good helper, don't I, Dad?"